VALERIE THOMAS AND KORKY PAUL

Winnie AND Wilbur

AROUND THE WORLD

OXFORD

UNIVERSITY PRESS

Winnie the Witch
and her big black cat Wilbur
were choosing their library books.

Well, Winnie was choosing them.
Wilbur just liked looking at the pictures.

Eathar

Emtenan

Hannah

Dooha

Adina

Humayra

Hassan

Thank you to Clifton Primary School,
Birmingham for helping with the endpapers.

For the fabulous Helen Mortimer—V.T.

To Brenda and Denis with love—K.P.

OXFORD
UNIVERSITY PRESS

Great Clarendon Street, Oxford OX2 6DP

Oxford University Press is a department of the
University of Oxford. It furthers the University's
objective of excellence in research, scholarship,
and education by publishing worldwide.
Oxford is a registered trade mark of
Oxford University Press in the UK and
in certain other countries

Text copyright © Valerie Thomas 2020
Illustrations copyright © Korky Paul 2020
The moral rights of the author and artist
have been asserted

Database right Oxford University Press (maker)

First published in 2020

British Library Cataloguing
in Publication Data available

ISBN: 978-0-19-277232-9 (hardback)

10 9 8 7 6 5 4 3 2 1

Printed in China

Paper used in the production of this book is a natural, recyclable
product made from wood grown in sustainable forests. The
manufacturing process conforms to the environmental
regulations of the country of origin

www.winnieandwilbur.com

Winnie was looking at a book
with lovely pictures of animals.

'Look at this beautiful giraffe,
Wilbur,' Winnie said.
'I've always wanted to see
a giraffe in the wild.'

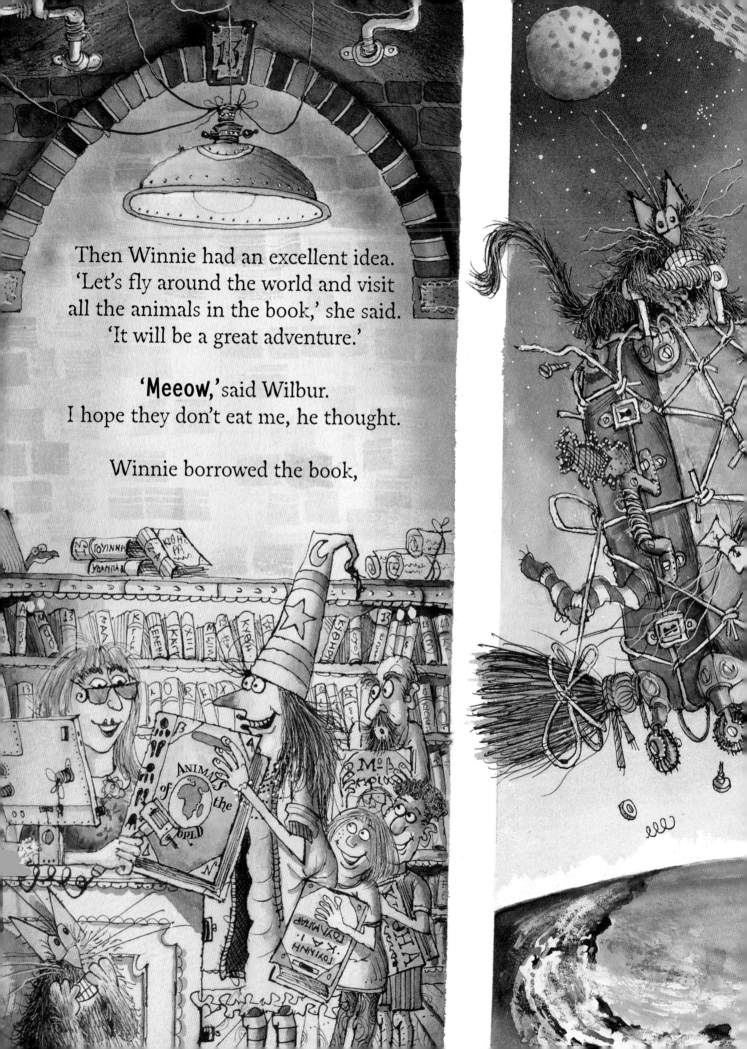

Then Winnie had an excellent idea.
'Let's fly around the world and visit
all the animals in the book,' she said.
'It will be a great adventure.'

'**Meeow,**' said Wilbur.
I hope they don't eat me, he thought.

Winnie borrowed the book,

flew home and packed their suitcase,
tied it to her broomstick,
and they zoomed up into the air.

Winnie looked at the first picture in
the book, then she waved her magic
wand, shouted,

'Abracadabra!'

and they were sitting in a tree house
watching some giraffes.
'We'll have our lunch,' Winnie said,
and she unpacked the sandwiches.

One of the giraffes walked over to look at them.
'Isn't it beautiful, Wilbur,' Winnie said.
'Look at its long eyelashes. And its long tongue.'

FLICK!

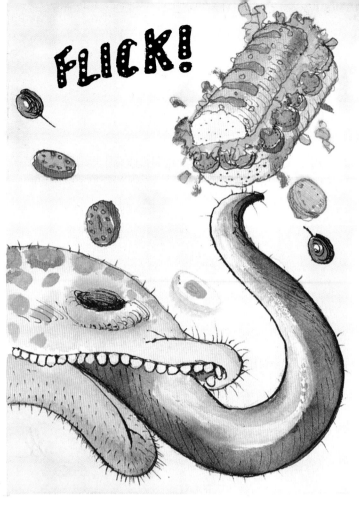

The sandwiches were gone.
But at least it didn't eat ME,
Wilbur thought.

Winnie looked
at the next picture.
She waved her wand, shouted,

'Abracadabra!'

and they landed at an oasis.

'Good!' said Winnie. 'I've always wanted to ride a camel across the desert.'

Winnie ate some dates and Wilbur drank camels' milk.

Then they joined a camel train and rode off across the desert, but it was very hot and the ride was bouncy.

Luckily Winnie still had her broomstick, so they climbed on and flew away.

The next picture in the book was . . .

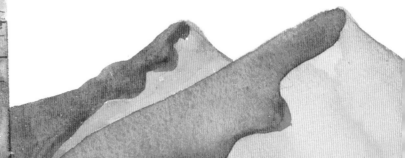

. . . kangaroos!

One of the kangaroos had a baby in her pouch.
Wilbur was interested in the pouch.

That's an excellent way to travel, he thought.

The baby kangaroo jumped out,
Wilbur jumped in, and the
kangaroo bounced away.

'Meeooow!'
cried Wilbur.

The mother kangaroo
looked into her pouch and
bounced back to Winnie.

Pandas were on the next page.

They ate bamboo,
rolled in the grass,
had a sleep, and
ate more bamboo.

Wilbur was happy to roll in the
grass and have a sleep, too.

But Winnie was bored.
'I hope the next animal
is a bit more exciting.'

Not too exciting,
Wilbur thought.

After the whale came a polar
bear and it looked hungry!
So Winnie and Wilbur didn't
land on the ice.

The next one was quite exciting.
An enormous whale!

It didn't want to eat Wilbur
but it was very splashy and
Wilbur hated getting wet.

Then they visited an elephant,
an aardvark, and some meerkats.

None of them ate cats.

'We are up to the last page now, Wilbur,' Winnie said.

She waved her wand, shouted,

'Abracadabra!'

and they were deep in the jungle,
surrounded by monkeys.

Naughty monkeys.

One of them pulled Wilbur's tail,
and another one grabbed
Winnie's wand, and . . .

threw it into the river
where a crocodile
snapped it up.

Luckily magic wands
taste horrible.

The crocodile spat out the wand,
and looked at Wilbur.

That cat looks much tastier, it thought.
It looked up at Wilbur and
opened its enormous mouth.

The crocodile was going to eat Wilbur!

'Meeeooow!' cried Wilbur.

Winnie grabbed Wilbur
and the wand, and they
zoomed up into the air.
'It's time to take this book
back to the library,'
Winnie said.

'But before we do,
you can choose
our very last animal,
Wilbur. Close your
eyes and think of your
favourite animal.

When you've thought of it,
I'll make a spell to take
us to where it lives.'

Wilbur closed his eyes
and thought about it.

Of course.
His favourite animal
was obvious.

Winnie waved her wand,
shouted,

'Abracadabra!'

and she was back in her
garden with Wilbur.

'You're my favourite animal,
too, Wilbur,' Winnie said.

'**Purr, purr, purr,**' said Wilbur.

Zara

Maya

Yasmine

Asmaa

Riyaan

Rumzee

Tasneem